MASCOT KIDS!
an imprint of Amplify Publishing Group

www.mascotbooks.com

Yanni the Yawning Yak

©2022 Ethan Pilkenton-Getty. All Rights Reserved. No part of this publication may be reproduced, stored in a retrieval system or transmitted in any form by any means electronic, mechanical, or photocopying, recording or otherwise without the permission of the author.

For more information, please contact:
Mascot Kids, an imprint of Amplify Publishing Group
620 Herndon Parkway, Suite 320
Herndon, VA 20170
info@mascotbooks.com

Library of Congress Control Number: 2022907360

CPSIA Code: PRT0822A

ISBN-13: 978-1-63755-324-4

Printed in the United States

YANNI THE YAWNING YAK

ETHAN PILKENTON-GETTY

Illustrated by iNDOS Studio

This is the story of Noah and how he learned that every animal is unique.

It all began one fateful evening when young Noah was tossing and turning in his bed having trouble getting to sleep. Right as Noah was starting to finally drift off to sleep, he heard a loud commotion in his backyard!

Noah curiously looked out his bedroom window and saw a strange-looking animal setting up a tent outside in the rain.

Noah opened the window and yelled, "Excuse me, what are you doing down there?"

The animal turned and replied, "Well hello, young man. Sorry to wake you. I was just traveling through and setting up camp for a quick night's sleep.

Excuse Me

My name is . . . my name is Yanni. Yanni the . . . YYYAAAKKK. Sorry. Yanni the Yak."

Noah replied, "You didn't wake me. Actually, I'm having trouble sleeping. And, you yawn funny!" Noah giggled.

Yanni was confused. "Is that so? And how am I supposed to yawn?"

YAWNNN

"Like everyone else does. Like this: YAWWWNNN."

"That's a great yawn!" Yanni excitedly shouted through his smile. "Can I let you in on a secret?" Yanni inquired.

"Okay! I love secrets! But let's get you out of the rain first," said Noah.

Once Noah and Yanni made it safely inside from the rain, Yanni began to tell Noah about his travels. "I come from far away, and I have traveled the world from end to end.

In my travels, I have seen some amazing things and met some amazing animals! And the secret I learned from all my travels is . . . that not all animals yawn the same way. They all yawn in their own unique and very special way. And that is what makes this world so wonderful and beautiful!"

Next is my friend Cairo the Camel. He is from Egypt, and he yawns like this:

EGYPT

Now you try and yawn like our friend Cairo!

Next is my friend Duggie the Dog. He is from England, and he yawns like this:"

DdaAWwgGg

ENGLAND

Now you try and yawn like our friend Duggie!

Next is my friend Gerry the Giraffe. She is from Namibia, and she yawns like this:

NAMIBIA

GgeErRaAfFf

Now you try and yawn like our friend Gerry!

HhiPpPoOo

Next is my friend Harriet the Hippo. She is from Kenya, and she yawns like this:"

KENYA

Now you try and yawn like our friend Harriet!

“Next is my friend Iggy the Iguana. He is from the Galapagos Islands, and he yawns like this:

Next is my friend Jasmine the Jaguar. She is from Mexico, and she yawns like this:

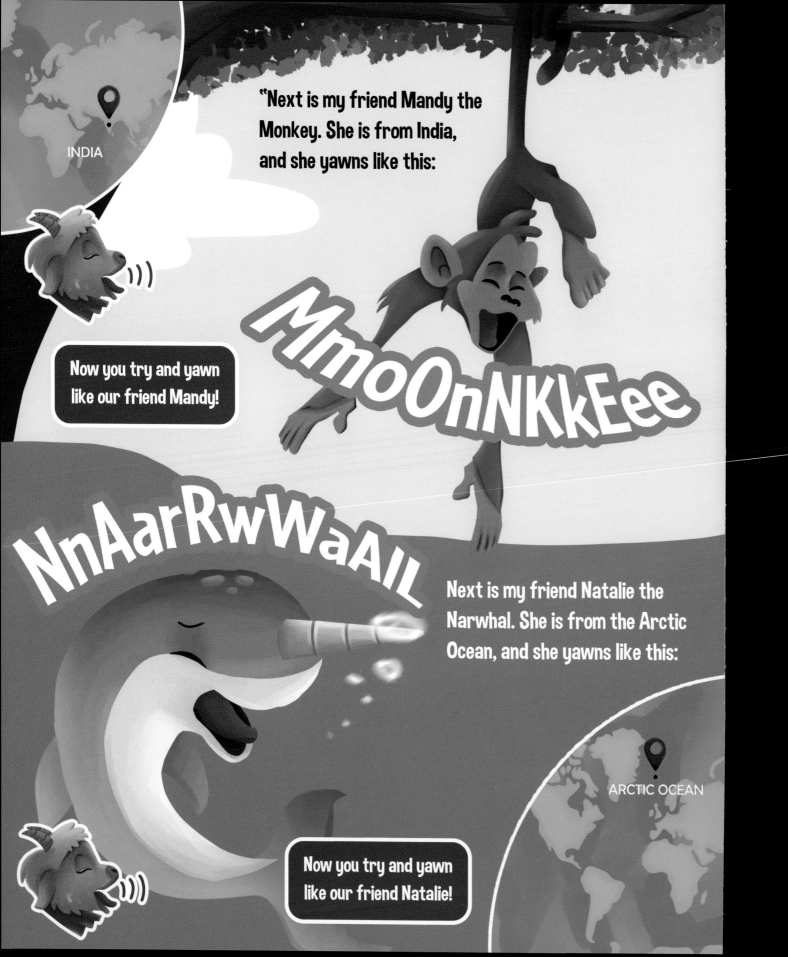

Next is my friend Sammy the Squid. He is from the Pacific Ocean, and he yawns like this:

PACIFIC OCEAN

Now you try and yawn like our friend Sammy!

SskKWWwwiiDd

Next is my friend Tommy the Toucan. He is from Costa Rica, and he yawns like this:"

TtoOkKaAnNh

COSTA RICA

Now you try and yawn like our friend Tommy!

HAWAII

"Next is my friend Ursula the Urchin. She is from Hawaii, and she yawns like this:

UurRCcHheEnN

Now you try and yawn like our friend Ursula!

Next is my friend Vinny the Viper. He is from Brazil, and he yawns like this:

VviiPpeErRr

Now you try and yawn like our friend Vinny!

BRAZIL

Next is my friend Wally the Whale. He is from the Atlantic Ocean, and he yawns like this:

ATLANTIC OCEAN

Now you try and yawn like our friend Wally!

wWhHaALleEe

Next is my friend Xena the X-ray Tetra Fish. She is from Venezuela, and she yawns like this:"

XxrRaAyYy

VENEZUELA

Now you try and yawn like our friend Xena!

Last but not least is my friend Zac the Zebra from South Africa. He yawns like this:"

ZzeEbBrRraAa

SOUTH AFRICA

Now you try and yawn like our friend Zac!

And that is the story of how Noah met his favorite Yak and how he learned about all the wonderful yawns around the world.

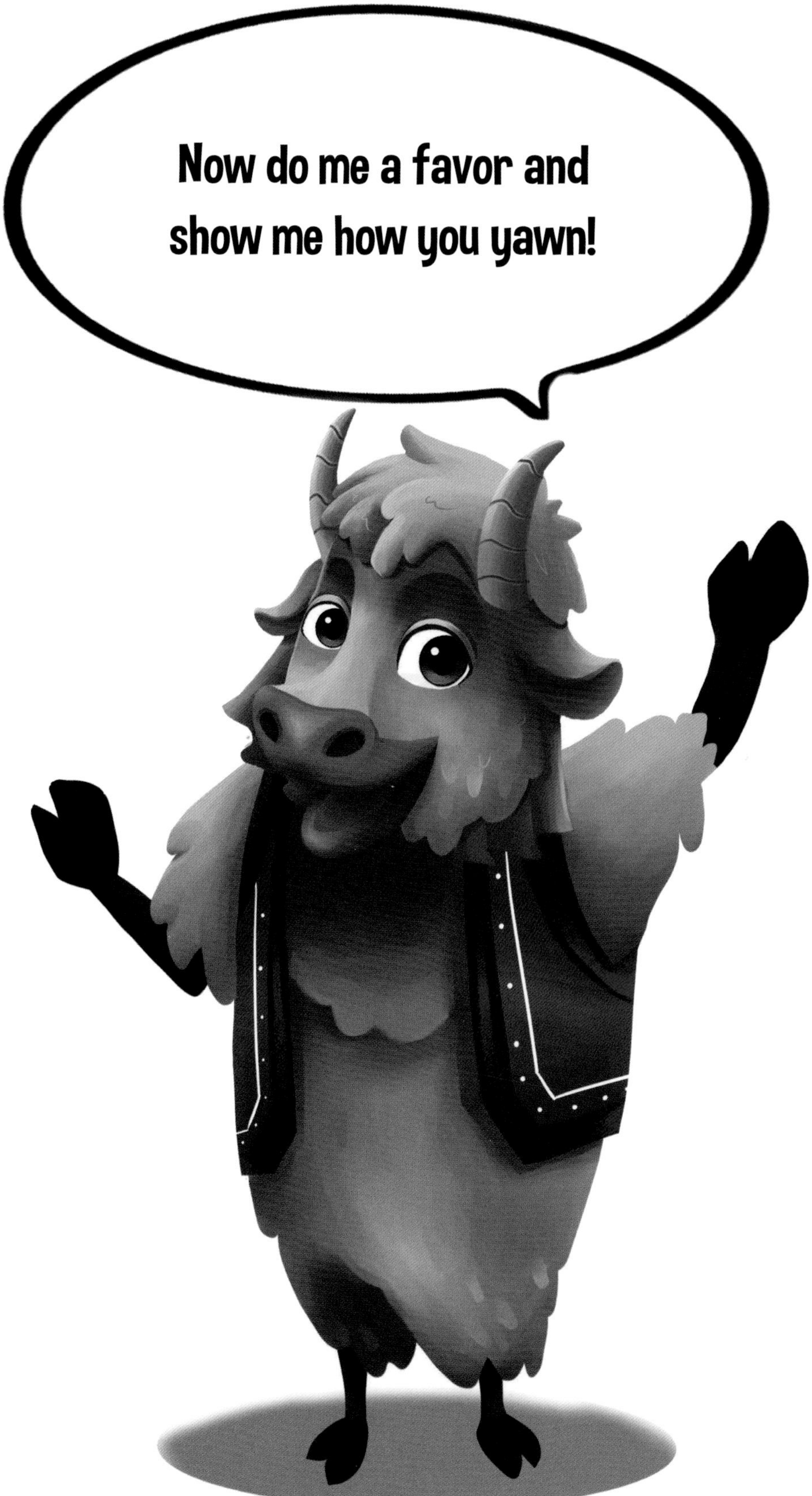
Now do me a favor and show me how you yawn!

About the Author

Ethan Pilkenton-Getty is an online business executive by day and a children's book writer by night. He was born and raised in a small coastal town in southern Maine and now resides in San Diego, California. He began writing his debut children's book after watching so many of his friends and family members read what seemed like countless books to their children before the little ones finally fell asleep. So he set out to help his exhausted friends by speeding up the bedtime routine and putting a couple more minutes back into their day. When Ethan is not writing or working, you can likely find him in the ocean pretending to know how to surf. He is a lover of the outdoors, adventure, travel, animals, and most of all—a good night's sleep.

Z z z